This book
belongs to:

D0417128

PIGLET

WINNIE THE POOH

EEYORE

STARRING

TIGGER

KANGA & ROO

OWL

RABBIT

This is a Parragon book
First published in 2006
Parragon
Queen Street House
4 Queen Street
Bath, BA1 1HE, UK

ISBN 1-40546-297-3
Printed in China

Copyright © 2006 Disney Enterprises, Inc.
Based on the "Winnie the Pooh" works by A.A. Milne and E.H. Shepard.
All rights reserved. No part of this publication may be
reproduced, stored in a retrieval system, or transmitted by
any means, mechanical, photocopying, recording or otherwise,
without the prior permission of the copyright holder.

Winnie the Pooh
and the
Blustery Day

It was one of those blustery days in the Hundred-Acre Wood and Winnie the Pooh was sitting in his thoughtful spot. This was his special place for sitting and thinking.

Pooh was wondering what to do when he suddenly thought, "Why, it's Windsday! This is my favourite day for visiting friends. I think I'll start with Piglet."

Piglet lived in a very fine house in a large beech tree. When Pooh arrived, Piglet was sweeping leaves away from the front door.

"I don't mind the leaves that that are leaving, it's the leaves that are coming that bother me," said Piglet.

"Happy Windsday, Piglet!" said Pooh, but Piglet didn't have time to say anything back to Pooh...

Just then, a gust of wind blew very hard and lifted Piglet into the air.

"Help me, Pooh," he cried.

Pooh made a grab but only caught the end of Piglet's scarf. The scarf began to unravel like a ball of string.

Piglet flew like a kite, while Pooh held on to one end of the scarf and ran as fast as he could go. Piglet flew over fields and hedges. They crashed right through Eeyore's house and Rabbit's carrot patch.

"Happy Windsday, Rabbit! Happy Windsday, Eeyore," shouted Pooh. Then an even bigger gust of wind lifted Pooh right off the ground.

The wind blew so hard that Pooh and Piglet blew right up to Owl's treetop home.

Owl saw them at the window, waving. He couldn't believe his eyes.

Very few of Owl's friends could climb so high up the tree, so it was a special treat for him to have visitors.

"Well!" said Owl. "This is a nice surprise! Do come in for a cup of tea."

He opened the window and Pooh and Piglet flew in.

"Happy Windsday, Owl!" said Pooh.

The wind was shaking Owl's house backwards and forwards.

Then it blew so hard that the house, with Owl, Pooh and Piglet inside, fell to the ground with a mighty CRASH!

All of their friends from the Hundred-Acre Wood came running to help.

"I don't think that we will ever be able to fix it," said
Christopher Robin, shaking his head. Eeyore was
shaking his head too.

"If you ask me," he said, "When a house looks like
that, it's time to find another one. It might take a day or
two, but I'll find one for you." Everyone thought that
this was a very good idea.

The friends sat around and waited and waited for Eeyore to return. It got later and later but still there was no sign of him. Christopher Robin yawned and decided that it was time for bed.

The very blustery day turned into a very blustery
night. Outside Pooh's house it rained and rained.
Inside Pooh had a very anxious sort of night filled
with anxious noises.

When Pooh woke up, the water was very deep and the Hundred-Acre Wood was flooded.

Pooh thought that he would eat some honey before it all floated away.

He was licking out the bottom of a honey pot when the water floated him right out of the door with his head stuck inside the pot.

When Piglet woke up he discovered water was coming in through the window. He wrote a note that read,

"HELP, ME, PIGLET".

Piglet put the note in a bottle and watched it float out of the window and out of sight. And then Piglet floated out of the window and out of sight.

Christopher Robin lived on a hill where the water could not reach. So that is where everyone from the Hundred-Acre Wood gathered.

Tigger, Rabbit, Kanga and Roo arrived in an umbrella. Owl was keeping watch from a tree. But there was no sign of Pooh and Piglet.

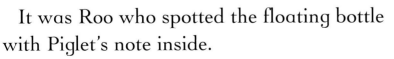

It was Roo who spotted the floating bottle with Piglet's note inside.

Christopher Robin read out the note and Owl flew off into the wood to search for Piglet.

"Tell him we'll rescue him as soon as we can," cried Christopher Robin.

As he flew over the flood, Owl saw Pooh and Piglet floating in the water. They were not far from Christopher Robin's hill. Piglet was standing on a chair and Pooh was still upside down in his honeypot.

Everyone was waiting at the edge of the water as Pooh and Piglet floated in.

"Well done, Pooh!" said Christopher Robin. "You've saved Piglet's life. You are a hero!"

"I am?" asked Pooh.

Christopher Robin said that as soon as the flood was over, he would give a hero's party for Pooh.

Finally, the rain stopped and Christopher Robin gave the hero's party. Everyone was there except Eeyore. He arrived late.

"I've found Owl a house," he said. "Follow me."

So they all followed Eeyore through the Hundred-Acre Wood. He led them right to Piglet's fine house in the beech tree.

Eeyore stood in front of Piglet's door and asked everyone to take a good look at Owl's fine new home. But everyone looked at Piglet.

"Well…" said Christopher Robin, "this is just the house for Owl. What do you think, Piglet?"

And then Piglet did a Noble thing.

"Yes," he said, "this is just the house for Owl and I hope he will be very happy in it."

Pooh looked at his little friend and whispered in Piglets ear, "That was a Noble thing you did."

Then Pooh said loudly, "Piglet, you can come and live with me."

So Christopher Robin gave a party for two heroes. Pooh was a hero for saving Piglet's life and Piglet was a hero for giving Owl a fine house.

Everyone had a lovely party and the blustery day
turned out to be not so bad after all.